DATE DUE			
	JAN 12 '95	NOV 9 '95	
FEB 3 1994 FEB 1 1994	JAN 26 '95	JAN 3 0 '95	
FEB 2 2 1994	JAN 26 '95	MAR 24 '97	
MAR 3 1994	FEB 21 '95	APR 7 '97	
	FEB 28 '95	APR 7 '97	
APR 2 8	MAR 9 '95	FEB 3 '99	
SEP 2 0 1994	MAR 21 '95	F. B 17 '0	
	APR 18 '95	AUG 31 '0	
OCT 4 1994	MAY 22 '95	NOV 19 '01	
DEC 21 '94		DEC 02 '02	
	OCT 1 1 '95		

E   Kraus, Robert, 1925-
Kra
           Here comes Tardy
           Toad

HERE COMES TARDY TOAD

BY ROBERT KRAUS

Silver Press

Library of Congress Cataloging-in-Publication Data

Kraus, Robert, 1925-
  Here comes Tardy Toad / by Robert Kraus.
    p. cm.—(Miss Gator's schoolhouse)
  Summary: All the animal students in Miss Gator's
school try to help Tardy Toad break his habit of
always being late to school, but their attempts have
a disastrous result.
  [1. Tardiness—Fiction. 2. Toads—Fiction.
3. Animals—Fiction. 4. Schools—Fiction.]
I. Title. II. Series: Kraus, Robert, 1925-
Miss Gator's schoolhouse.
PZ7.K868Hef   1989
[E]—dc20   89-10222
                                                     CIP
ISBN 0-671-68607-0   AC
ISBN 0-671-68611-9 (pbk.)

Produced by Parachute Press, Inc.
Copyright © 1989 by Robert Kraus.
All rights reserved. No part of this book may be used
or reproduced in any manner whatsoever without written
permission from the publisher.
Published by Silver Press, a division of
Silver Burdett Press, Inc.
Simon & Schuster, Inc.,
Prentice Hall Bldg., Englewood Cliffs, NJ 07632.
Printed in the United States of America.
10 9 8 7 6 5 4 3 2 1

Chapter 1
ALL ABOUT TARDY

Tardy Toad came from a long

line of tardy toads.

His father was tardy.

His mother was tardy.

His uncle on his mother's side
was tardy.

His aunt on his father's side
was tardy.

And so were his grandmothers

and grandfathers.

On both sides.

"I come by my tardiness naturally," said Tardy Toad. But Miss Gator would have none of it.

"You must learn to be on time," she said when Tardy Toad arrived—late as usual.

"How can we help Tardy get to
school on time?" Miss Gator
asked the class.

"I go to bed early,"

said Miss Gator.

"What do you all do?"

12

"My mom and dad set my
alarm clock for me,"
said Ella the Bad Speller.
"They make sure I leave for
school on time."

"I don't dawdle on the way to school," said Blake the Snake.

"I polish my boots and lay out
my clothes the night before,"
said Punky Skunky.

"And I always sleep with my
clothes on," said Buggy Bear.
"We know," said the class.
"We know!"

"I hope this has given you lots of ideas for getting to school on time, Tardy," said Miss Gator.

"It sure has," said Tardy.
"I'm going to be on time
tomorrow, or my name isn't…"

"TARDY TOAD!" said the class.

So that night, Tardy
went to bed early.

Chapter 2
TARDY TRIES

He set six alarm clocks.

And he wore his hat to bed.

But Tardy Toad could not

fall asleep.

He could not fall asleep...

and could not fall asleep...

and could not fall asleep!

The sun came up,

and still poor Tardy

could not fall asleep.

At 6 A.M. sharp, Tardy's

alarm clocks all went off.

BRRRRRRRRRRRING!

BRRRRRRRRRRRING!

BRRRRRRRRRRRING!

BRRRRRRRRRRRING!

BRRRRRRRRRRRING!

BRRRRRRRRRRRING!

And at last, Tardy Toad

fell asleep.

Fast asleep!

ZZZZZZZZZZZZZZZZZZZZZZZZZZZZZZZZZZ

Tardy's mother and father were
fast asleep too.

It looked like Tardy would be
tardy again.
But then...

There was a knocking at
Tardy's door!
"Wake up, Tardy,"
said Ella the Bad Speller,
Buggy Bear, Blake the Snake,
and Punky Skunky.
"Wake up! Wake up!"
they cried.
"You're going
to be late."

"Huh? Who? Wha...t?"

mumbled Tardy.

Chapter 3
HELPING TARDY

Blake and Ella pulled Tardy out
of bed.

Blake the Snake made his bed.

In two shakes.

Buggy Bear showed him

how to wash up.

Fast.

Ella the Bad Speller
quickly checked his homework
for spelling mistakes.
Punky Skunky made him
a quick breakfast.

"Hurry," hissed Blake.

"'Don't dawdle!"

"I'm hurrying!
I'm hurrying!" said Tardy,
tripping over his feet.

Then they all hopped
on Tardy's raft
and headed for school.

They had not gone far
when the raft
came to a sudden stop.

"We're stuck in the mud!"

hissed Blake.

"We're on the rocks!"

cried Buggy.

"We're sinking!"

said Ella the Bad Speller.

"S-I-N-K-I-N-K!"

"Abandon raft!"

shouted Blake the Snake.

"And don't dawdle!"

Tardy Toad and the class
jumped into the swamp
and waded to school.

"I'm all wet," said Ella.

"You're not kidding,"

said Blake the Snake.

Across the swamp at the little
red schoolhouse, Miss Gator
was ringing the schoolbell.
CLANG! CLANG! CLANG!

44

"I can't believe it,"
said Miss Gator.
"They're ALL tardy!"

At last the class arrived.

"I'm sorry we're late,

Miss Gator," said Tardy.

"Everyone was trying to help

me get to school on time."

"That's all right,"
said Miss Gator.
"At least you tried.
And it's never too late
to try again."

Then the whole class got
cleaned up.
It was time to begin another day
at Miss Gator's schoolhouse.